The Adventures of CAPTAIN UNDERPANTS

TRA-LA-LAAAA!

The First Epic Novel by
DAV PILKEY

THE BLUE SKY PRESS
An Imprint of Scholastic Inc. • New York

For David and Nancy Melton
with gratitude

THE BLUE SKY PRESS

Copyright © 1997 by Dav Pilkey
All rights reserved.
No part of this publication may be reproduced, stored
in a retrieval system, or transmitted in any form or by any means,
electronic, mechanical, photocopying, recording, or otherwise,
without written permission of the publisher.
For information regarding permission, please write to:
Permissions Department, Scholastic Inc.,
557 Broadway, New York, New York 10012.
SCHOLASTIC, THE BLUE SKY PRESS, and associated logos are
trademarks and/or registered trademarks of Scholastic Inc.
ISBN 0-439-75668-5
10 9 8 7 6 5 4 3 2 1   05 06 07 08 09
Printed in China   62
First Collectors' Edition printing, September 2005

Sturgeon General's Warning:

Some material in this book may be
considered offensive by people
who don't wear underwear.

CHAPTERS

CHAPTER 1
GEORGE AND HAROLD

Meet George Beard and Harold Hutchins.
George is the kid on the left with the tie
and the flat-top. Harold is the one on the
right with the T-shirt and the bad haircut.
Remember that now.

George and Harold were best friends. They had a lot in common. They lived right next door to each other and they were both in the same fourth-grade class at Jerome Horwitz Elementary School.

George and Harold were usually responsible kids. Whenever anything bad happened, George and Harold were usually responsible.

But don't get the wrong idea about these two. George and Harold were actually very nice boys. No matter what everybody else thought, they were good, sweet, and lovable. . . . Well, OK, maybe they weren't so sweet and lovable, but they were good nonetheless.

It's just that George and Harold each had a "silly streak" a *mile* long. Usually that silly streak was hard to control. Sometimes it got them into trouble. And once it got them into big, *BIG* trouble.

But before I can tell you that story, I have to tell you *this* story.

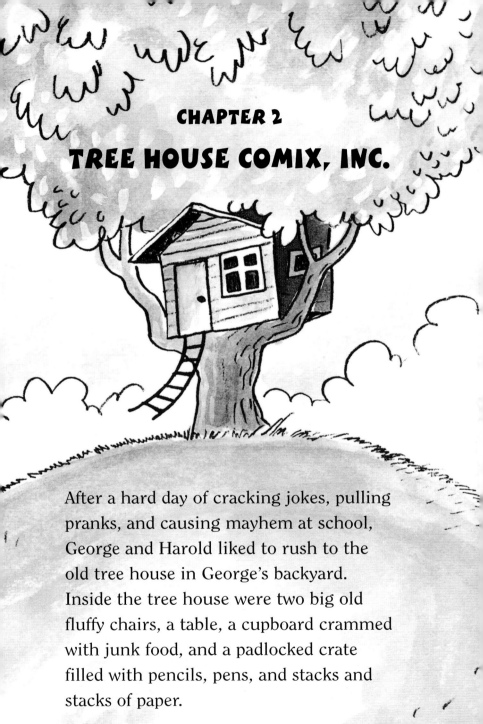

CHAPTER 2
TREE HOUSE COMIX, INC.

After a hard day of cracking jokes, pulling
pranks, and causing mayhem at school,
George and Harold liked to rush to the
old tree house in George's backyard.
Inside the tree house were two big old
fluffy chairs, a table, a cupboard crammed
with junk food, and a padlocked crate
filled with pencils, pens, and stacks and
stacks of paper.

Now, Harold loved to draw, and George loved to make up stories. And together, the two boys spent hours and hours writing and drawing their very own comic books.

Over the years, they had created hundreds of their own comics, starring dozens of their own superheroes. First there was "Dog Man," then came "Timmy the Talking Toilet," and who could forget "The Amazing Cow Lady"?

But the all-time greatest superhero they ever made up *had* to be "The Amazing Captain Underpants."

George came up with the idea.

"Most superheroes *look* like they're flying around in their underwear," he said. "Well, this guy actually *is* flying around in his underwear!"

The two boys laughed and laughed.

"Yeah," said Harold, "he could fight with *Wedgie Power*!"

George and Harold spent entire afternoons writing and drawing the comic adventures of Captain Underpants. He was their coolest superhero ever!

Luckily for the boys, the secretary at Jerome Horwitz Elementary School was much too busy to keep an eye on the copy machine. So whenever they got a chance, Harold and George would sneak into the office and run off several hundred copies of their latest Captain Underpants adventure.

After school, they sold their homemade comics on the playground for 50¢ each.

CHAPTER 3

THE ADVENTURES OF CAPTAIN UNDERPANTS

WRitten By George Beard
Cartoons By Harold Hutchins

Don't Miss our Next
Exsiting Adventure:

CAPTAIN UNDERPANTS
and the
ATTACK OF THE
TALKING TOILETS

COMING Soon to A
PLAYground Near You.

TREEHOUSE
COMIX, INC.

CHAPTER 4

MEAN OLD MR. KRUPP

Do you see that old guy
looking out the window
up there?
That's Mr. Krupp,
the principal.

Now, Mr. Krupp was the meanest, sourest old principal in the whole history of Jerome Horwitz Elementary School. He hated laughter and singing. He hated the sounds of children playing at recess. In fact, he hated children altogether!

And guess which two children Mr. Krupp hated most of all?

If you guessed George and Harold, you're right! Mr. Krupp *hated* George and Harold.

He hated their pranks and their wise-cracks. He hated their silly attitudes and their constant giggling. And he especially hated those awful *Captain Underpants* comic books.

"I'm going to get those boys one day," Mr. Krupp vowed. "One day very, very soon!"

CHAPTER 5

ONE DAY VERY, VERY SOON

Remember when I said that George and Harold's "silly streak" got them into big, *BIG* trouble once? Well, this is the story of how that happened. And how some huge pranks (and a little blackmail) turned their principal into the coolest superhero of all time.

It was the day of the big football game between the Horwitz Knuckleheads and the Stubinville Stinkbugs. The bleachers were filled with fans.

The cheerleaders ran onto the field and shook their pom-poms over their heads.

A fine black dust drifted out of their pom-poms and settled all around them.

"Gimme a K!" shouted the cheer-leaders.

"*K!*" repeated the fans.

"Gimme an N!" shouted the cheer-leaders.

"*N!*" repeated the fans.

"Gimme an . . . a-ah-ah-A-CHOO!" sneezed the cheerleaders.

"*A-ah-ah-A-CHOO!*" repeated the fans.

The cheerleaders sneezed and sneezed and sneezed some more. They couldn't stop sneezing.

"Hey!" shouted a fan in the bleachers. "Somebody sprinkled black pepper into the cheerleaders' pom-poms!"

"I wonder who did that?" asked another fan.

The cheerleaders stumbled off the field, sneezing and dripping with mucus, as the marching band members took their places.

But when the band began to play, steady streams of bubbles began blowing out of their instruments! Bubbles were *everywhere*! Up and down the field the marching band slipped and slid, leaving behind a thick trail of wet, bubbly foam.

"Hey!" shouted a fan in the bleachers. "Somebody poured bubble bath into the marching band's instruments!"

"I wonder who did that?" asked another fan.

Soon, the football teams took the field. The Knuckleheads kicked the ball. Up, up, up went the ball. Higher and higher it went. The ball sailed into the clouds and kept right on going until nobody could see it anymore.

"Hey!" shouted a fan in the bleachers. "Somebody filled the game ball with *helium*!"

"I wonder who did that?" asked another fan.

But the missing ball didn't make any difference because at that moment, the Knuckleheads were rolling around the field, scratching and itching like crazy.

"Hey!" shouted the coach. "Somebody replaced our Deep-Heating Muscle Rub Lotion with Mr. Prankster's Extra-Scratchy Itching Cream!"

"We wonder who did that?!" shouted the fans in the bleachers.

The whole afternoon went on much the same way, with people shouting everything from "Hey, somebody put Sea-Monkeys in the lemonade!" to "Hey, somebody glued all the bathroom doors shut!"

Before long, most of the fans in the bleachers had gotten up and left. The big game had been forfeited, and everyone in the entire school was *miserable*.

Everyone, that is, except for two
giggling boys crouching in the shadows
beneath the bleachers.

"Those were our best pranks yet!"
laughed Harold.

"Yep," chuckled George, "they'll be
hard to top, that's for sure."

"I just hope we don't get busted for
this," said Harold.

"Don't worry," said George. "We
covered our tracks really well. There's
no way we'll get busted!"

CHAPTER 6
BUSTED

The next day at school, an announcement came over the loudspeakers.

"George Beard and Harold Hutchins, please report to Principal Krupp's office at once."

"Uh-oh!" said Harold. "I don't like the sound of *that*!"

"Don't worry," said George. "They can't prove anything!"

George and Harold entered Principal Krupp's office and sat down on the chairs in front of his desk. The two boys had been in this office together countless times before, but this time was different. Mr. Krupp was *smiling*. As long as George and Harold had known Mr. Krupp, they had never, *ever* seen him smile. Mr. Krupp knew something.

"I didn't see you boys at the big game yesterday," said Mr. Krupp.

"Uh, no," said George. "We weren't feeling well."

"Y-Y-Yeah," Harold stammered nervously. "W-W-We went home."

"Aw, that's too bad," said Principal Krupp. "You boys missed a good game."

George and Harold quickly glanced at each other, gulped, and tried hard not to look guilty.

"Lucky for you, I have a videotape of the whole thing," Mr. Krupp said. He turned on the television in the corner and pressed the play button on the VCR.

A black-and-white image appeared on the TV screen. It was an overhead shot of George and Harold sprinkling pepper into the cheerleaders' pom-poms. Next came a shot of George and Harold pouring liquid bubble bath into the marching band's instruments.

"How do you like the *pre-game show*?" asked Mr. Krupp with a devilish grin.

George eyed the television screen in terror. He couldn't answer. Harold's eyes were glued to the floor. He couldn't look.

The tape went on and on, revealing all of George and Harold's "behind the scenes" antics. By now, both boys were eyeing the floor, squirming nervously, and dripping with sweat.

Mr. Krupp turned off the TV.

"You know," he said, "ever since you boys came to this school, it's been one prank after another. First you put dissected frogs in the Jell-O salad at the parent-teacher banquet. Then you made it snow in the cafeteria. Then you rigged all the intercoms so they played "Weird Al" Yankovic songs *full blast* for six hours straight.

"For *four long years* you two have been running amok in this school, and I've never been able to prove anything—until now!"

Mr. Krupp held the videotape in his hand. "I took the liberty of installing tiny video surveillance cameras all around the school. I knew I'd catch you two in the act one day. I just didn't know it would be *so easy!*"

CHAPTER 7
A LITTLE BLACKMAIL

Mr. Krupp sat back in his chair and chuckled to himself for a long, long time. Finally, George got up the courage to speak.

"W-What are you going to do with that tape?" he said.

"I thought you'd never ask," laughed Principal Krupp.

"I've thought long and hard about what to do with this tape," Mr. Krupp said. "At first, I thought I'd send copies to your parents."

The boys swallowed hard and sank deeply into their chairs.

"Then I thought I might send a copy to the school board," Mr. Krupp continued. "I could get you both *expelled* for this!"

The boys swallowed harder and sank deeper into their chairs.

"Finally, I came to a decision," Mr. Krupp concluded. "I think the football team would be very curious to find out just *who* was responsible for yesterday's fiasco. I think I'll send a copy to them!"

George and Harold leaped out of their chairs and fell to their knees.

"No!" cried George. "You can't do that. They'll *kill* us!"

"Yeah," begged Harold, "they'll kill us every day for the rest of our lives!"

Mr. Krupp laughed and laughed.

"Please have mercy," the boys cried. "We'll do anything!"

"Anything?" asked Principal Krupp with delight. He reached into his desk, pulled out a list of demands, and tossed it at the boys. "If you don't want to be *dead as long as you live,* you'll follow these rules *exactly!"*

George and Harold carefully looked over the list.

"This . . . this is blackmail!" said George.

"Call it what you like," Principal Krupp snapped, "but if you two don't follow that list *exactly*, then this tape becomes the property of the Horwitz Knuckleheads!"

#22

#13

#7. NO

RULES

#1. NO MORE PRACTICAL JOKES OR PRANKS

#2. NO LAUGHING OR SMILING

#3. NO MORE T

#4. NO MORE CAPTAIN UNDERP

#5. WASH MY CAR EVER

#6. MOW MY

CHAPTER 8

CRIME AND PUNISHMENT

At six o'clock the next morning, George and Harold dragged themselves out of bed, walked over to Mr. Krupp's house, and began washing his car.

Then, while Harold scrubbed the tires, George roamed around the yard pulling up all the weeds and crabgrass he could find. Afterward, they cleaned the gutters and washed all the windows on Mr. Krupp's house.

At school, George and Harold sat up straight, listened carefully, and spoke only when spoken to. They didn't tell jokes, they didn't pull pranks—they didn't even smile.

Their teacher kept pinching herself. "I just *know* this is a dream," she said.

At lunch, the two boys vacuumed
Mr. Krupp's office, shined his shoes,
and polished his desktop. At recess, they
clipped his fingernails and ironed his tie.

Each spare moment in the boys' daily
schedule was spent catering to Mr.
Krupp's every whim.

41

After school, George and Harold mowed Mr. Krupp's lawn, tended his garden, and began painting the front of his house. At sunset, Mr. Krupp came outside and handed each boy a stack of books.

"Gentlemen," he said, "I've asked your teachers to give you *both* extra homework. Now go home, study hard, and I'll see you back here at six o'clock tomorrow morning. We've got a busy day ahead of us."

"Thank you, sir," moaned the two boys.

George and Harold walked home dead tired.

"Man, this was the worst day of my entire life," said George.

"Don't worry," said Harold. "We only have to do this for eight more years. Then we can move away to some far-off land where they'll never find us. Maybe Antarctica."

"I've got a better idea," said George.

He took a piece of paper out of his
pocket and handed it to Harold. It was an
old magazine ad for the 3-D Hypno-Ring.

"How's *this* going to help us?" asked
Harold.

"All we gotta do is hypnotize Mr.
Krupp," said George. "We'll make him
give us the video and forget this whole
mess ever happened."

"That's a great idea!" said Harold. "And
the best part is we only have to wait four-
to-six weeks for delivery!"

44

CHAPTER 9

FOUR-TO-SIX WEEKS LATER

After four-to-six weeks of backbreaking slave labor, grueling homework assignments, and humiliating good behavior at school, a package arrived in George's mailbox from the Li'l Wiseguy Novelty Company.

It was the 3-D Hypno-Ring.

"Hallelujah!" cried George. "It's everything I ever hoped for!"

"Let me see, let me see," said Harold.

"Don't look directly at it," warned George. "You don't want to get hypnotized, do you?"

"Do you really think it will work?" asked Harold. "Do you really think we can 'amaze our friends, control our enemies, and take over the world' just like the ad says?"

"It better work," said George. "Or else we just wasted four whole bucks!"

CHAPTER 10

THE 3-D HYPNO-RING

The next morning, George and Harold
didn't arrive early at Mr. Krupp's house
to wash his car and reshingle his roof. In
fact, they were even a little late getting to
school.

When they finally showed up, Mr.
Krupp was standing at the front door
waiting for them. And boy, was he *mad*!

Mr. Krupp escorted the boys into his office and slammed the door.

"All right, where were you two this morning?" he growled.

"We wanted to come over to your house," said George, "but we were busy trying to figure out the secret of this *ring*."

"What ring?" snapped Mr. Krupp.

George held up his hand and showed the ring to Principal Krupp.

"It's got one of those weird patterns on it," said Harold. "If you stare at it long enough, a picture appears."

"Well, hold it still," snarled Mr. Krupp. "I can't see the darn thing!"

"I have to move it back and forth," said George, "or else it won't work."

Mr. Krupp's eyes followed the ring back and forth, back and forth, back and forth, and back and forth.

"You have to stare deeper into the ring," said Harold. "Deeper . . . deeeper . . . deeeeper . . . deeeeeeeeeper."

"You are getting sleepy," said George. "Veeeeery sleeeeeeeeeepy."

Mr. Krupp's eyelids began to droop. "I'mmmsssoooosssleeepy," he mumbled.

After a few minutes, Mr. Krupp's eyes were closed tight, and he began to snore.

"You are under our spell," said George. "When I snap my fingers, you will obey our every command!"

Snap!

"Iwwilllloobeyyy," mumbled Mr. Krupp.

"All right," said George. "Have you still
got that videotape of me and Harold?"

"Yeeessss," mumbled Mr. Krupp.

"Well, hand it over, bub," George
instructed.

Mr. Krupp unlocked a large file cabinet
and opened the bottom drawer. He
reached in and handed George the videotape. George stuffed it into his backpack.

Harold took a *different* video out of his
backpack and put it into the file cabinet.

"What's that video?" asked George.

"It's one of my little sister's old
'Boomer the Purple Dragon Sing-A-Long'
videos."

"Nice touch," said George.

CHAPTER 11

FUN WITH HYPNOSIS

When Harold bent down to close the file cabinet, he took a quick look inside.

"Whoa!" he cried. "Look at all the stuff in here!"

The file cabinet was filled with everything Mr. Krupp had taken away from the boys over the years. There were slingshots, whoopee cushions, skateboards, fake doggy doo-doo—you name it, it was in there.

"Look at this!" cried George. "A big stack of *Captain Underpants* comics!"

"He's got every issue!" said Harold.

For hours, the two boys sat on the floor laughing and reading their comics. Finally, George looked up at the clock.

"Yikes!" he said. "It's almost lunchtime! We better clean up this mess and get to class."

The boys looked up at their principal, who had been standing behind them in a trance all morning.

"Gee, I almost forgot about Mr. Krupp," said Harold. "What should we do with him?"

"Do you want to have some fun?" asked George.

"Why not?" said Harold. "I haven't had *any* fun in the last four-to-six weeks!"

"Cool," said George. He walked up to Mr. Krupp and snapped his fingers. *Snap!* "You are—a *chicken*!" he said.

Suddenly, Mr. Krupp leaped onto his desk and flapped his arms. "Cluck, cluck, cluck-cluck," he cried, kicking his papers off the desk behind him and pecking at his pen-and-pencil set.

George and Harold howled with laughter.

"Let me try, let me try," said Harold.

"Ummm, you are a—a *monkey*!"

"You gotta snap your fingers," said
George.

"Oh, yeah," said Harold. *Snap!* "You
are a *monkey*!"

Suddenly, Mr. Krupp sprang off his
desk and began swinging from the
fluorescent light fixtures. "Ooo-ooo, ooo-
oooo, OOOOO!" he shrieked, leaping from
one side of the room to the other.

George and Harold laughed so hard
they almost cried.

"My turn, my turn!" said George. "Let's see. What should we turn him into next?"

"I know," Harold said, holding up a *Captain Underpants* comic. "Let's turn him into Captain Underpants!"

"Good idea," said George. *Snap!* "You are now the greatest superhero of all time: *The Amazing Captain Underpants*!"

Mr. Krupp tore down the red curtain from his office window and tied it around his neck. Then he took off his shoes, socks, shirt, pants, and his awful toupee.

"Tra-La-Laaaaaaaa!" he sang.

Mr. Krupp stood before them looking quite triumphant, with his cape blowing in the breeze of the open window. George and Harold were dumbfounded.

"You know," said George, "he kinda *looks* like Captain Underpants."

"Yeah," Harold replied.

After a short silence, the two boys looked at each other and burst into laughter. George and Harold had never laughed so hard in all their lives. Tears ran down their faces as they rolled about the floor, shrieking in hysterics.

After a while, George pulled himself up from the floor for another look.

"Hey," George cried. "Where'd he go?"

CHAPTER 12
OUT THE WINDOW

George and Harold dashed to the window
and looked out. There, running across the
parking lot, was a pudgy old guy in his
underwear with a red cape flowing
behind him.

TRA-LA-LAAA!

"Mr. Krupp, come back!" shouted Harold.

"He won't answer to *that*," said George. "He thinks he's Captain Underpants now."

"Oh, no," said Harold.

"He's probably runnin' off to fight crime," said George.

"Oh, *no,*" said Harold.

"And we gotta stop him," said George.

"Oh, NO," cried Harold. *"NO WAY!"*

"Look," said George, "he could get *killed* out there."

Harold was unmoved.

"Or worse," said George. "We could get into BIG trouble!"

"You're right," said Harold. "We *gotta* go after him!"

The two boys opened the bottom file-cabinet drawer and took out their slingshots and skateboards.

"Do you think we should bring anything else?" asked Harold.

"Yeah," said George. "Let's bring the fake doggy doo-doo."

"Good thinking," said Harold. "You just never know when fake doggy doo-doo is going to come in handy!"

Harold stuffed Mr. Krupp's clothes, shoes, and toupee into his backpack. Then together the two boys leaped out the window, slid down the flagpole, and took off on their skateboards after the Amazing Captain Underpants.

CHAPTER 13
BANK ROBBERS

George and Harold rode their skateboards all over town looking for Captain Underpants.

"I can't find him anywhere," said Harold.

"You'd think a guy like him would be *easy* to spot," said George.

Then the boys turned a corner, and *there* he was. Captain Underpants was standing in front of a bank, looking quite heroic.

"Mr. Krupp!" cried Harold.

"Shhh," said George, "don't call him that. Call him Captain Underpants!"

"Oh, yeah," said Harold.

"And don't forget to snap your fingers," said George.

"Right!" said Harold.

RRRRiiiiiNNNG

ALARM

But before he got a chance, the bank doors flew wide open, and out stepped two robbers. The robbers took one look at Captain Underpants and stopped dead in their tracks.

"Surrender!" said Captain Underpants. "Or I will have to resort to *Wedgie Power!*"

"Oh, no," whispered Harold and George.

Nobody moved for about ten seconds. Finally, the robbers looked at each other and burst out laughing. They dropped their loot and fell to the sidewalk screaming in hysterics.

Almost immediately, the cops showed up and arrested the crooks.

"Let that be a lesson to you," cried Captain Underpants. "Never underestimate the power of underwear!"

The police chief, looking quite angry, marched over to Captain Underpants.

"And just who the heck are *you* supposed to be?" the police chief demanded.

"Why, *I'm* Captain Underpants, the world's greatest superhero," said Captain Underpants. "I fight for Truth, Justice, and *all* that is Pre-Shrunk and Cottony!"

"Oh, *YEAH*!!?" shouted the police chief. "Cuff him, boys!"

One of the cops took out his handcuffs and grabbed Captain Underpants by the arm.

"Uh-oh!" cried George. "We gotta roll!"
Together the two boys zoomed into the
crowd, weaving in and out of cops and
bystanders. Harold skated up to Captain
Underpants and knocked the superhero
off his feet. George caught him and the
boys skated away with Captain
Underpants on their shoulders.

"Stop!" cried the cops, but it was too
late. George, Harold, and Captain
Underpants were gone.

CHAPTER 14

THE BIG BANG

After their quick escape, George, Harold, and Captain Underpants stopped on a deserted street corner to catch their breath.

"OK," said George. "Let's de-hypnotize him quick, before something else . . .

. . . happens!"

A huge explosion came from the Rare Crystal Shop across the street. Heavy smoke poured out of the building. Suddenly, two robots with one stolen crystal emerged from the smoke and jumped into an old van.

"Did I just see two *ROBOTS* get into a van?" asked Harold.

"You know," said George, "up until *now* this story was almost *believable!*"

"Well, believable or not," said Harold, "we're not getting involved. I repeat: We are *NOT* getting involved!"

Just then, Captain Underpants leaped from the street corner and dashed in front of the van.

"Stop, in the name of underwear!" he cried.

"Uh-oh," said George. "I think we're *involved*."

The two robots started up the van and swerved around Captain Underpants. Unfortunately, the van brushed up against his red cape, and it got caught. With a mighty *jerk*, Captain Underpants flipped backward, and the van pulled him along as it drove away.

"GRAB HIM!" cried George.

The two boys skateboarded with all
their might toward the speeding van and
grabbed Captain Underpants by the
ankles.

"HEEEEEEELLLLLLLP!" they cried
as the van pulled them through the
city streets.

"Mommy," said a little boy sitting on a bench, "I just saw two robots driving a van with a guy in his underwear hanging off the back by a red cape, pulling two boys on skateboards behind him with his feet."

"How do you expect me to believe such a ridiculous story?" asked his mother.

Finally, the van came to a screeching halt in front of an old abandoned warehouse. The sudden stop made Captain Underpants flip over the roof of the van and crash through the front door of the building.

"Well, well, well," said a strange voice from inside the warehouse. "It looks as if we have a *visitor*."

CHAPTER 15
DR. DIAPER

George and Harold hid behind the van until the coast was clear. Then they sneaked up to the hole in the door and peeked inside.

Captain Underpants was all tied up, the two robots were standing guard, and a strange little man wearing a diaper was laughing maniacally.

"I am the evil Dr. Diaper," the strange
little man told Captain Underpants. "And
you will be the first to witness my
takeover of the *world*!"

Dr. Diaper placed the stolen crystal
into a large machine called the *Laser-
Matic 2000*. The machine started to light
up and make loud noises. Heavy gears
began shifting and spinning, and a laser
beam from the crystal shot straight up
through a hole in the roof.

"In exactly twenty minutes, this laser beam will blow up the moon and send huge chunks of it crashing down upon every major city in the world!" laughed Dr. Diaper. "Then, I will rise from the rubble and take over the planet!"

"Only one thing can help us now," said George.

"What?" asked Harold.

"Rubber doggy doo-doo," said George.

Harold took the fake doggy doo-doo and a slingshot from George's backpack and handed them to him.

"Be careful," said Harold. "The fate of the entire planet is in your hands!"

With careful and precise aim, George shot the rubber doo-doo through the air and across the room. It landed with a *plop!*—right at the feet of Dr. Diaper.

"Yessss!" whispered George and Harold.

Dr. Diaper looked down at the doo-doo between his feet and turned bright red.

"Oh, dear me!" he cried. "I'm dreadfully embarrassed! Please excuse me."

He began to waddle toward the rest-room. "This has never happened to me before, I assure you," he said. "I-I guess with all the excitement, I just . . . I just. . . . Oh, dear! Oh, dear!"

While Dr. Diaper was off changing himself, George and Harold sneaked into the old warehouse.

Immediately, the robots detected the boys and began marching toward them. "Destroy the intruders!" said the robots. "Destroy the intruders!"

George and Harold screamed and ran to the back of the warehouse. Luckily, George found two old boards and gave one of them to Harold.

"We're not going to have to resort to extremely graphic violence, are we?" asked Harold.

"I sure hope not," said George.

CHAPTER 16

THE EXTREMELY GRAPHIC VIOLENCE CHAPTER

WARNING:

The following chapter contains graphic scenes showing two boys beating the tar out of a couple of robots.

If you have high blood pressure, or if you faint at the sight of motor oil, we strongly urge you to take better care of yourself and stop being such a baby.

PILKEY® BRAND
‑RAMA

HERE'S HOW IT WORKS!

Step 1

Place your *left* hand inside the dotted lines marked "LEFT HAND HERE." Hold the book open *flat*.

Step 2

Grasp the *right-hand* page with your right thumb and index finger (inside the dotted lines marked "RIGHT THUMB HERE").

Step 3

Now *quickly* flip the right-hand page back and forth until the picture appears to be *animated*.

(For extra fun, try adding your own sound-effects!)

FLIP-O-RAMA 1

(pages 83 and 85)

Remember, flip *only* page 83.
While you are flipping, be sure you
can see the picture on page 83
and the one on page 85.
If you flip quickly, the two
pictures will start to look like
<u>one</u> *animated* picture.

Don't forget to
add your own sound-effects!

LEFT HAND HERE

ROBOT RAMPAGE!

RIGHT THUMB HERE

84

ROBOT RAMPAGE!

FLIP-O-RAMA 2

(pages 87 and 89)

Remember, flip *only* page 87.
While you are flipping, be sure you
can see the picture on page 87
and the one on page 89.
If you flip quickly, the two
pictures will start to look like
<u>one</u> *animated* picture.

Don't forget to
add your own sound-effects!

LEFT HAND HERE

GEORGE SAVES HAROLD!

RIGHT
THUMB
HERE

88

GEORGE SAVES HAROLD!

FLIP-O-RAMA 3

(pages 91 and 93)

Remember, flip *only* page 91.
While you are flipping, be sure you
can see the picture on page 91
and the one on page 93.
If you flip quickly, the two
pictures will start to look like
<u>one</u> *animated* picture.

Don't forget to
add your own sound-effects!

LEFT HAND HERE

HAROLD RETURNS
THE FAVOR!

RIGHT
THUMB
HERE

HAROLD RETURNS
THE FAVOR!

FLIP-O-RAMA 4

(pages 95 and 97)

Remember, flip *only* page 95.
While you are flipping, be sure you
can see the picture on page 95
and the one on page 97.
If you flip quickly, the two
pictures will start to look like
<u>one</u> *animated* picture.

Don't forget to
add your own sound-effects!

LEFT HAND HERE

MIXED NUTS (...AND BOLTS!)

RIGHT
THUMB
HERE

96

MIXED NUTS
(...AND BOLTS!)

CHAPTER 17

THE ESCAPE

After defeating the robots, George and
Harold untied Captain Underpants.

"Come on!" cried Harold. "Let's get out
of here!"

"Wait!" said Captain Underpants. "We
have to save the world first!"

So George, Harold, and Captain
Underpants frantically looked all over the
Laser-Matic 2000, searching for a way
to shut it down and stop the inevitable
disaster.

"Ummm," said Harold. "I think *this* might be the lever we want."

He pulled the "Self-Destruct" lever with all his might. Suddenly, the *Laser-Matic 2000* began to sputter and shake. The huge laser beam turned off, and pieces of the machine began flying off in all directions.

"It's gonna BLOW!" cried Harold. "RUN FOR YOUR LIVES!"

"NOT SO FAST!" screamed Dr. Diaper, who had appeared out of nowhere. "You demolished my robots. You *destroyed* my *Laser-Matic 2000*. And you ruined my one chance to take over the world—but you won't live to tell the tale!" Dr. Diaper pulled out his *Diaper-Matic 2000* ray gun, and pointed it at George, Harold, and Captain Underpants.

Captain Underpants quickly stretched a pair of underwear and shot it at Dr. Diaper. The underwear landed right on the evil doctor's head.

"Help!" cried Dr. Diaper. "I can't see! I can't see!"

George and Harold ran out of the warehouse as fast as they could.

"Great shot, Captain Underpants!" cried Harold.

"There's just one thing I don't understand," said George. "Where'd you get the *extra* pair of underwear?"

"What extra pair?" said Captain
Underpants.

"Never mind that," cried George, "let's just get out of here before that *Laser-Matic 2000* thing ex . . .

. . . plodes!"

The *Laser-Matic 2000* blew up, tearing apart the old warehouse. It sent flaming shards of red-hot metal in every direction. Fire fell from the skies around our heroes, and the earth began to crumble beneath their feet.

"Oh, NO!" cried Harold. *"WE'RE DOOMED!"*

CHAPTER 18

TO MAKE A LONG STORY SHORT

They got away.

CHAPTER 19

BACK TO SCHOOL

George, Harold, and Captain Underpants
made a quick stop outside the police
station. They tied Dr. Diaper to a lamp-
post and attached a note to him.

"There!" said Captain Underpants.
"That ought to explain everything."

Then George and Harold led Captain
Underpants back to Jerome Horwitz
Elementary School.

"Why are we going *here*?" asked
Captain Underpants.

"Well," said George, "you have to do
some *undercover* work here."

"Yeah," said Harold, reaching into his
backpack. "Put these clothes on, and
make it snappy!"

"Don't forget your hair," said George.

Captain Underpants quickly got
dressed behind some bushes. "Well, how
do I look?" he asked.

"Pretty good," said George. "Now try
to look really mad!"

Captain Underpants made the nastiest
face he could.

"You know," said Harold, "he kinda
looks like Mr. Krupp!"

"*Harold,*" whispered George, "he is
Mr. Krupp!"

"Oh, yeah," said Harold. "I almost
forgot."

Before long, they were all back inside
Mr. Krupp's office.

"OK, Captain Underpants," said
George, "you are now Mr. Krupp."

"Snap your fingers," whispered Harold.

"Oh, yeah," said George. *Snap!* "You
are now Mr. Krupp."

"Who's Mr. Krupp?" asked Captain
Underpants.

"Oh, NO!" cried Harold. *"It's not
working!"*

The boys tried again and again to
de-hypnotize Captain Underpants, but
nothing seemed to work.

"Hmmm," said Harold. "Let me see the instruction manual for that ring."

George checked his pants pockets.

"Umm," said George, "I think I *lost* it."

"You WHAT?" cried Harold. The two boys searched frantically through the office, but the 3-D Hypno-Ring instruction manual was nowhere to be found.

"Never mind," said George. "I have an idea." He removed the flowers from a large vase in the corner. Then he poured out all of the water over Captain Underpants's head.

"What did you do *that* for?" cried Harold.

"I saw 'em do this in a cartoon once," said George, "so it's *gotta* work!"

After a few minutes, Mr. Krupp slowly came to. "What's going on here?" he demanded. "And why am I all wet!!?"

George and Harold had never been so glad to see Mr. Krupp in all their lives.

"I'm so happy I could cry," said Harold.

"Well, you're *gonna* cry when I give that videotape to the football team!" shouted Mr. Krupp. "I've *had it* with you two!"

Principal Krupp took the videotape
out of his file cabinet. "You boys are *dead
meat!*" he sneered. He stormed out of his
office with the video and headed toward
the gym.

George and Harold smiled. "Wait'll the
football team sees *that* video!" said
Harold.

"Yeah," said George, "I sure hope they
like singing purple dragons!"

115

"Hey, look," said George. "I found the 3-D Hypno-Ring instruction manual. It was in my *shirt* pocket, not my pants pocket!"

"Well, throw that thing away," said Harold. "We'll never need it again."

"I sure hope not," said George.

WARNING!!!
Whatever you do, don't pour water on anybody's head when they are in a trance! This will cause the hypnotized person to slip back and forth from trance to reality whenever they hear the sound of fingers snapping.

TRASH

CHAPTER 20

THE END?

♪ LA-LA-LA-LA- WE LOVE BOOMER-LA-LA

Things at Jerome Horwitz Elementary
School were never quite the same after
that fateful day.

The football team enjoyed Mr. Krupp's
video so much that they changed their
name from the Knuckleheads to the
Purple Dragon Sing-A-Long Friends. The
name change didn't go over too well with
the fans, but hey, who's going to argue
with a bunch of linebackers?

George and Harold went back to their old ways, pulling pranks, cracking jokes, and making new comic books.

They had to keep an eye on Mr. Krupp, though . . .

. . . because for some *strange* reason,
every time he heard the sound of fingers
snapping . . .

Snap!

. . . Principal Krupp turned *back* into . . .

. . . *you know who*!

"Oh, no!" cried Harold.
"Here we go *again*!" said George.

ABOUT THE AUTHOR

When Dav Pilkey was in elementary school, he was always getting into trouble for pulling pranks, cracking jokes, and making silly comic books. In second grade, he invented his most famous (or infamous) character, CAPTAIN UNDERPANTS!

Dav's teacher told him, "You'd better straighten up, young man, because you can't spend the rest of your life making silly books."

Luckily for us, Dav was not a very good listener! His Captain Underpants books are all national bestsellers and have been translated into numerous languages. Dav also wrote and illustrated *Dog Breath*, winner of the California Young Reader Medal; *The Paperboy*, a Caldecott Honor Book; and the IRA-CBC Children's Choice Award-winning Dumb Bunnies books. His popular Ricky Ricotta's Mighty Robot series, illustrated by Martin Ontiveros, continues to thrill young readers. Dav and his dog live in Eugene, Oregon.

Be sure to check out Dav Pilkey's Extra-Crunchy Web Site O' Fun at www.pilkey.com, and also visit www.scholastic.com/captainunderpants.

HAVE YOU READ YOUR UNDERPANTS TODAY?

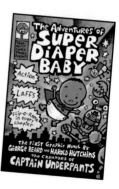

CD-ROM SYSTEM REQUIREMENTS

WINDOWS®

- Pentium® 233 MHz processor
- Windows® 98/Me/2000/XP
- 128 MB RAM
- Windows® compatible sound card and speakers
- 640x480 resolution color display
- 4X speed multi-session CD-ROM drive or CD-RW/DVD-ROM drive
- Mouse
- Minimum browser requirements: Safari™ 1.0, Microsoft Internet Explorer® 3.x, Netscape Navigator® 3.x

MACINTOSH®

- 400 MHz PowerPC® processor
- System 10 (OSX)
- 128 MB RAM
- 640x480 resolution color display
- 4X speed multi-session CD-ROM drive or CD-RW/DVD-ROM drive
- Mouse
- Minimum browser requirements: Safari™ 1.0, Microsoft Internet Explorer® 3.x, Netscape Navigator® 3.x